M. Kelly Peach

The
Death of
Tintagiles
Death

A Novella

Copyright © 2024 M. Kelly Peach

All rights reserved. No part of this publication may be reproduced, distributed, or transmitted in any form or by any means, including photocopying, recording, or other electronic or mechanical methods, without the prior written permission of the publisher, except in the case of brief quotations embodied in critical reviews and certain other noncommercial uses permitted by copyright law.

Front cover image/ interior design by:

ANXIETY DRIVEN GRAPHICS

ISBN: 9798334789159

TEP

Ygraine: So we will talk no more about the things we cannot know…

Maurice Maeterlinck, *The Death of Tintagiles, Act 1*

The child Tintagiles' head is cradled lovingly in his cupped hands—so strong and skillful—as he gouges his thumbs to the first knuckles into the eye sockets. With Aglovale, the aged guard, he had to go even deeper, almost to the second knuckle of each thumb but not so deep for the sisters Ygraine and Bellangère.

He picks up an eight-inch boxwood knife and, cutting deeply, slashes Tintagiles' mouth with it. Switching to a Duron sculpting tool, he presses the sulfur-free plasticine from the mouth slit to form plump upper and lower lips. Cocking his head right and then left, while tilting the clay head, gives the artist the necessary perspectives for envisioning Tintagiles' face. A slight cleft in the lower lip is needed. He takes up a boxwood tool with a sharp 60-degree angled head and, with delicate touch, creates it.

To free his hands, he inserts a sharpened ¼ inch diameter nine-inch long dowel rod into the marionette's head just under what will be the chin and clamps it to his work desk. As he stares at the beige, over-sized mango with a mouth and two deep pits for eyes, he absently cleans the sculpting tools with a rag and returns them to the correct position in their respective rows on the stainless steel surgical Mayo tray on his workbench. Even though his eyes have never left the plasticine head, he is nevertheless aware the boxwood knife's placement was slightly askew and reaches out to straighten it.

A lump the shape and size of an official hacky-sack bag is taken from what remains of the two pound Del Milano modeling clay brick and, after warming it in his hands, is placed above the mouth and formed into a broad nose with generous nostrils. This, he knows, will play better on the stage than the patrician's thin bridge and narrow nostrils he would have preferred for Tintagiles' noble character.

Two lumps of clay, with the swift and sure ministrations of the puppet sculptor's hands, are magically transformed into ears and affixed, in their proper locations, to the head. They appear too flat so, using his fingers only, he adjusts them to stick out a bit more.

Two more dollops of clay are removed from the dwindling brick. They are shaped into identical peach stones and placed into the eye sockets.

He spends another hour forming the face. Material has to be removed to form cheekbones, chin, forehead, etc. During the process two no-filter Camels and half of a half-full tumbler of Old Grand-Dad are consumed. There is a burning in his throat, familiar and comfortably uncomfortable, with each swallow of whiskey and—from the cigarette in his mouth—in his eyes whenever he tilts his head while shaping. The plasticine shavings are collected and added back to the remains of the brick.

The artist stands back several feet and examines the finished product. He moves to the right side of it then the left, sometimes stooping, other times standing on tip toe, to look at it from every angle. He is pleased with how the model is, so far, capturing the essential childishness of Tintagiles.

In a sardonic salute qua toast, he raises the tumbler to his newest character then drains it. He refills the glass—an eleven-ounce Anchor Hocking rocks, an oddity one occasionally sees with a square bottom morphing into a circular top (the last of his deceased mother's collection)—from the gallon jug of what he affectionately terms Old Gob-Smack. He only ever bothers with ice cubes when he has company over; can't remember the last time he had visitors.

After clearing space on his work bench and covering it with old newspapers, he removes the plastic covering of an off brand, discount, roll of white paper towel and tosses it into the nearby waste basket. He begins meticulously tearing off curved strips about two inches long and half an inch wide. With an ample supply of strips piled high on the work desk, he gets out the chipped and stained cereal bowl he uses for pasting. Preferring a thick, smooth, and better smelling papier-maché adhesive, he eschews the cheaper, odorous cook method of one part flour and five parts water and opts for equal parts Elmer's white, all-purpose glue—also kept in a gallon jug—and water.

The first piece of maché is submerged in the paste and then placed, as is his custom, over the bridge of the model's nose like it is some sort of sticky Breathe Right nasal strip. He remembers when they first came out. His wife insisted he try this revolutionary new product as a possible solution to his heavy-machinery-hard-at-work snores. He informed her they wouldn't work but, rather than continuing to argue the point and risk an escalation into pitched battle, as so often happened between them, went along and gave it a try. Her disappointment the next morning, he recalled, was bitter. She was certain he had, in some way, while sleeping, sabotaged the experiment, just to prove his point. She insisted he try it again. He acquiesced, again—another of his customs—but his snoring was still at the level of a one hundred car freight train rolling through town.

The next day, with the morning sunshine streaming through the bedroom window and songbirds singing in the yard, she was, if possible, even more bitter. She insisted he try again because with practice he would eventually get it right and cease his snoring. The television commercials for Breathe Right clearly implied their wonderful product reduced snoring to the gentlest of zephyrs.

He refused. This resulted in another in a long series of fragile and friable détentes in their decades-long, sometimes cold war of a marriage.

They loved each other very much but were too often, like two superpowers locked into a relationship, suspicious and paranoid and constantly maneuvering for the upper-hand. Without the slightest clue as to details, he knows he will be pre-emptively charged and eventually found guilty of violating the cease-fire through some inadvertent remark or unspecified but very much necessary action he failed to accomplish.

Working quickly, he covers the head with the viscid strips meticulously overlapping them. He uses his fingers and boxwood tools, preferring the spatula and ball shaped instruments, to tuck the strips along all the planes and into every crevice of Tintagiles' face while being very careful to never puncture the papier maché. The process is repeated with four more layers. Most puppeteers stop with four layers but he likes the added strength and durability of five.

The paper towel strips for the fifth and final layer are placed with painstaking precision. Every edge is secured. When completely covered, he applies a final thin coat of the paste using a long flat, size 10 Winton Hog Brush.

He washes his hands. The bowl and all of his tools are cleaned, dried and put back in their proper places. The work bench is tidied before he kills the lights and leaves for upstairs. With a de-humidifier in the laundry room next to the workshop operating at maximum, the head should be dry in about twenty-four hours.

Still wired from his spate of creativity, he decides to unwind with one more coffin nail, another gurgling boost from Grandpa, and an episode from his favorite television show. He gets out his boxed set of *The Twilight Zone: The Complete Definitive Collection* and starts going through the twenty-eight DVDs trying to find a good one he hasn't seen in a while. As far as he is concerned, they're all good and *TZ* is the greatest show in the history of television but certain episodes, like *Caesar and Me*, *The Dummy*, *The After Hours*, and *The Living Doll*, all of which feature mannequins, dummies and dolls coming to life, are too frightening so he skips past those and settles for one of his paranoiac favorites: *The Monsters Are Due on Maple Street.* The disc is slipped into the eager slot of the player. He settles on the couch as a black and white Rod Serling—lipless, gaunt but with killer eyebrows, deadly serious, and cigarette in hand—introduces the twenty-second episode of the first season.

Most towns in America do have a Maple Street so it's not surprising this viewer is a resident of one himself. As Claude Akins and his McCarthyistic neighbors become increasingly schizoid, the long day, not to mention the alcohol, begin to take effect and he drowsily wonders about his own neighbors, all of whom, other than to wave at and say hello, are virtual strangers. With bourbon and butt consumed, he drifts into slumber as the remaining episodes on the disc play out to the background noise of a backhoe with a bad muffler.

※ ※ ※

The next day he takes up Tintagiles' head and, as he has with all of the marionette characters he's created, begins lightly sanding it smooth with 220 grit fine sandpaper. He finishes the sanding and wipes the head clean before applying a base coat of casein-lime wall paint he has mixed to a healthy, slightly peach-colored hue. Tintagiles is clamped again to the work desk so the paint can dry.

※ ※ ※

The next day the puppet's eyes are painted with oil-based titanium white. While they are drying, the puppet-maker applies a very light shade of rose lake to the cheeks, lips and nostrils then brushes in the eyebrows with gold ochre. He breaks for some nicotine and rotgut; not because he needs it, just something to do while he gives the paint time to dry. He is not an alcoholic and can quit anytime.

After break, his hands are still steady enough to paint the black pupils and circle them with irises of a rich terre verte shade hinting at turquoise. It is time for another break, another opportunity for the delicious scorching of eyes and throat as he examines his artistry and is much pleased. Although his Tintagiles is older than Maeterlinck's, the face is still naïf and child-like, but with subtle, underlying lines of strength and purpose.

The paint has dried; time for trepanning the puppet. Starting at the base of the skull, he takes a utility knife and slices through the papier maché following a large, penciled-in oval. He imagines Tintagiles' face, resting securely in his cupped left hand, scrunches in pain as he cuts but that has to be the whiskey, as it sometimes will, playing games with his brain. The section of skull, at the first careful attempt at removal, is stuck and requires additional cutting. He hears a groan; must be the old coal burning octopus furnace—converted to natural gas thirty years ago—making noises again. With delicacy and deliberation, the second attempt is successful and the back of the head is set off to the side of the workbench.

To scoop out the modeling clay, he uses a tarnished, Victorian-era silver plate sugar spoon (classic shell pattern by Wm. Rogers and Son) purchased by his mother for twenty-five cents at a garage sale many years ago. It is the only silver spoon he, or anybody else in his family, has ever owned.

When approximately half the clay, some of it showing folds and convolutions not there when he was sculpting (must be from the drying process), is dug out the rest emerges neatly, to his immense satisfaction, and is returned to the Del Milano clay.

Tintagiles needs a moveable mouth so the puppet-maker starts with a cut separating the upper lip from the lower. At the edge of each side of the mouth he slices straight down and then under the chin. Again, the furnace is moaning in pain.

These two cuts are joined by deftly tracing the curve of the top of the throat with the utility knife. The lower lip with chin section is removed and placed on the work bench. He gets out his pasting bowl and a one pound can of DAP Plastic Wood. After prying off the lid, he discovers he is running low but has enough to finish the project. He fills the bowl half-full with water. Wetting his fingers first, he scoops out a dab of DAP and forms into a biscuit which is then placed into the inside point of the chin and down into the throat. More of the plastic wood is applied to the interior of the rest of the face and head to strengthen and reinforce the papier-maché. Wetting his fingers again, he presses the material into all the contours. Again, he dips his fingers in the bowl and then gets more plastic wood for another coating inside the chin and to fill the entire throat. He makes sure enough DAP is applied so that he can, after it dries, install the speaking apparatus.

Time to call it a day, actually a night; he cleans his hands and bowl, dries them, clamps the puppet's head to its place at the work desk, clears his bench area, gets his booze and white, soft pack of dromedaries, turns off the light, and goes upstairs to watch television.

✗ ✗ ✗

Next morning, he completes the chin apparatus. bolt screwed into the throat area thus keeping the mouth closed until the puppeteer needs This delicate work requiring great skill allows the marionette to speak.

For Tintagiles trunk, he starts with a 6" X 3" X 3" pine block for the shoulder and chest section. He cuts it down to child-sized proportions and uses inch thick dowel rods for the arms and legs which are connected with muslin at the shoulders and hips. The wrists and ankles are ball and socket joints; the elbows and knees are hinge joints using strips of twelve or thirteen-ounce Sole Bend armor leather. He finishes the leather hinges for the other knee and both elbows then attaches the head to the body. Tired, he decides to stop for the night and carries Tintagiles to the storage cabinet to hang on a hook next to the other marionettes. Before closing the door, he steps back and examines the proportions of the limbs in relation to the head. He assumes one of his favored poses with right arm close to the body, forearm resting on his stomach and right hand cupping the left elbow. His left hand is positioned with the edge facing out, the thumb along the jaw line and the middle knuckle of the forefinger nestled in the philtrum. Ostensibly, the idea is to appear pensive and ruminative. If you can't look handsome try to look intelligent. The true, underlying, and unspoken purpose has always been to hide as much as possible the loathsome disfigurations of his chin and below his mouth.

Tintagiles' head is slightly large relative to the limbs and this is exactly the effect he wanted. Already thinking about how he will carve the hands and feet starting tomorrow, he closes the cabinet door which, rubbing against the frame, makes a sound similar to a frightened, sharp intake of breath.

On the way upstairs, he grabs his bottle of Gramps, empty tumbler, and pack of filterless fags. Instead of television tonight, he's thinking about listening to music and deciding which tape to play.

※ ※ ※

Late next morning, after some dry toast, a mug of coffee and several ibuprofen, he is using a 1" X 3" pine block and a jig saw to quickly cut first the left and then the right foot for Tintagiles. The feet will be covered in slippers so all he has to do is rough in the shape.

For the hands, he uses another block of pine. It takes him the rest of the day to carve, chisel, whittle and sand them into shape. They are remarkably lifelike with fingernails, knuckles, and the veins on the back of the hands painstakingly detailed. He is more than pleased with the quality of the work considering these are the first ones he has ever done with only nine fingers.

The right hand, like father...like son, has its index finger missing and is formed to a grasping configuration; the left has a slight lifting of the index finger with the other three fingers curled under to give a semblance of life and vigor. He paints them the same hue used for the face and gives the veins a bluish tint.

Later, after the paint has dried, standing in front of his work space, he sucks flame into his nineteenth ship of the desert for the day then places his hands on the edge of the work bench and leans in for a close and final inspection of the finished products lying there. Through the bluish stinging fumes, looking at the marionette's hands and then his own hands, he sees he has, without intending to, created man hands instead of child hands.

Shrugging, he decides audience members probably won't notice. Examining the stub of the right index finger with care, he grins with approval thinking the application of rose lake to the tip is a nice touch and a rather close approximation to his own recently healed remnant of right index finger.

He pours himself another drink before tackling the job of attaching the hands to wrists. The glass, unwashed in at least two weeks and looking a little gray and filmy, is only a quarter full. His immediate reaction is anger at whoever has been drinking his bourbon and then realizes, with a goofy grin, it's only been him. Purchase of more booze takes precedence so he goes upstairs for his jacket and wallet.

Walking to the liquor store, he self-talks about the need for his best behavior otherwise the clerk might, like he has in the past, refuse to sell to him. After several blocks and some serious inner-debate he comes to the pleasant conclusion he should buy a quart each of Jack Daniel's Tennessee whiskey and Old Grand-Dad.

At the store, he's well behaved and the clerk is happy to sell him both bottles of golden surcease. He hurries home to work on the marionette and, incidentally, replenish his cocktail.

Back in his basement workshop, relishing the sipid, gingerline scorch, he attaches small eye bolts to the hands and sets them down to open the eye bolts already installed in the ends of the dowel rods acting as Tintagiles' combined radiuses and ulnas. This accomplished, it is time for a break and another sip or two and the lighting and inhalation of a white, tobacco-filled tube of death.

Respite time finished and not wanting to repeat the embarrassing mix up with the feet, he is careful to attach the right hand to the right arm and close up the eye bolt with a squeeze of needle nose pliers. When he repeats this operation with the left arm and hand, the tool slips from the head of the bolt and somehow bangs the stump of his right index finger on the top of the work bench. He simultaneously flings the pliers and lurches to his feet knocking his work stool backwards, then goes into a back-and-forth jig of pain while sucking on his excruciated nubbin.

With all the bleary concentration he can muster, he finishes the connection for the left forelimb. During the process, it almost seemed like Tintagiles was moving both of his left arms to keep his two wrists in alignment with the pair of carved hands held in Kyle's trembling fingers. He actually had to close one eye to bring wrist and hand into focus and reduce them to their correct number.

The puppet-maker decides to call it a night and returns the nearly completed marionette to its cabinet. It takes him three attempts to get the figure correctly positioned on the tricky bastard of a hook that, despite two screws fastening it to the back wall, keeps moving—first right, then left. When he closes the cabinet door it again makes an unusual sound which barely registers to his besotted brain. This time it is less the frightened intake of breath as before and more a resigned exhalation.

⚔ ⚔ ⚔

The next day Kyle calls the Artistic Director and explains he is almost finished with Tintagiles and would like to work on the wig and clothes. She gives him permission to skip rehearsals for *Sleeping Beauty,* a show he's done hundreds of times, to finish the title character for their next show, a new production of an old marionette play by Maurice Maeterlinck called *The Death of Tintagiles*, scheduled for late May. Connie knows he has already finished the figures for the other three characters: Ygraine, Bellangére, and Aglovale but he is cutting it close for the title character. Rehearsals start next week for this masterpiece of Maeterlinck's. She is nervous because it's a play of existentialist doom for adults and the Detroit Puppet Company usually does kid-friendly productions; she is also very excited about the opportunity for her troupe, several of whom were classically trained in St.

Petersburg, to stretch and give flight to their artistic wings.

He decides to try the Salvation Army Thrift stores first and strikes gold, as it were, when he finds a vintage Bell curly blonde wig for a Shirley Temple doll at the shop on Fort Street. The $2 wig is at least thirty years old and was hiding on a shelf behind a jumble of dolls including a nude, headless Barbie, a Cabbage Patch with no arms, and a plastic clown doll with one blue, working eye open and the other broken eye closed so it appeared to be winking a come-hither look of skin crawling creepiness.

He checks in the children's clothing section for a usable night shirt and pair of slippers but finds nothing to his liking so, after paying for the wig, he decides to try the Michigan Avenue store.

At the Michigan Avenue shop he finds a vintage French christening gown. The white, fine cotton garment with scalloped embroidery has to be at least seventy years old but is in pristine condition and is only ten bucks. With some simple alterations it should work fine as a night shirt. With the left-over cotton he plans to create three strings the shape and length of linguine and drape them over the neck and wrists to give it an authentic Victorian-era appearance.

It's his lucky day because he finds a pair of white, child's cloth slippers in the shoe section. They are only two dollars and will have to be cleaned but should fit nicely over Tintagiles' feet. The display case next to the cash register is filled with an assortment of pen knives, costume jewelry, Zippo and Roston lighters, ceramic figures, U.S. Army and Boy Scout compasses, mismatched and tarnished pieces of silverware, cork screws and dozens of other items of dubious worth. His eye catches a silver letter opener shaped as a dagger. The blade has intricate scroll-like engravings and is about 9" long. The crescent-shaped cross guard is heavy and also engraved; the grip is mother-of-pearl and the pommel is a silver lozenge. It will be perfect as Aglovale's sword.

He purchases his finds and departs for home. On the way there he stops at a liquor store, the windows and doors secured by black steel bars like one might see at a maximum-security prison, and purchases a fifth of Maker's Mark. He plans to celebrate when his last, finest marionette is finished.

At home he goes to the basement right away and sets his bags on the work bench and gets out the wig. It only takes him about twenty minutes to comb out some of the curls and trim others so that the wig is looking the way it should for a near-pubescent boy.

The prepared wig is placed on Tintagiles' head. The fit is almost perfect so it takes only a few adjustments to get it correctly aligned. Kyle carefully peels back the front edge of the hair piece and applies white Elmer's to the netting and sticks it to the top of the forehead. He does the same to both temples and the back of the head.

While the glue is drying he ingests some amber throatburn then gets to work on the gown soon to be nightshirt. From costuming well over a hundred marionettes in the past thirty years, his skills as a tailor are considerable. By the end of the evening—with precise measurements, deft work of his shears, and much hand-stitching—he has Tintagiles wearing a well-fitted, authentic-looking nightshirt with strings at throat and wrists.

He is very tired and a little tipsy but is determined to finish the job by stringing the puppet to its controller.

He has several used ones stored away in an ancient, battered file cabinet drawer next to the bench. After some rummaging he finds an old favorite. It is in the shape of a patriarchal cross and was used many years ago for a production of *Pinocchio*. Also in the drawer is a new favorite string he started using in the last few years: a white, braided fifty-pound test fishing line. He quickly attaches the strings to controller and puppet.

He holds the *fantoche* in his hands at arm's length; left supporting the head and neck, right the back of the thighs and, like any new parent, gazes in wonder and love as he carries his son to the cupboard. After hanging Tintagiles to his hook, Kyle steps back and stares in admiration of this, his last and finest creation. Its beauty is ethereal, numinous.

The marionette's remarkably lifelike head—more so than any other figure he's ever done—lolls to the left and his thin chest seems to rise and fall with respiration but that of course is a stray air current moving the night shirt although it is odd the bottom of the garment is still. As Kyle is closing the cupboard door, Tintagiles' head changes balance and tips to the right which motion gives it the appearance of sadness or perhaps a gesture of negation.

On the way upstairs he grabs the numbing bottle with the red wax and finds a clean glass in the kitchen cupboard on the way to the music room. Setting bottle and glass on the end table, he is thinking about tunes from all the young dudes: Overend, Buffin, Mick, Verden, and their leader Ian—poet laureate of Oswestry.

Kyle fires up the tape deck, puts on a pair of black framed Gazelle shades, pours himself a stiff one, lights a lung-slayer, and plugs in *Mad Shadow*. The band, fierce and fearless, rocks it loose and loud, low and sweet, while the vocalist, graveled and Dylanesque, sings from a gutter, divinely.

He relaxes into the embrace of his easy chair, swallows a finger's worth of golden fire, puffs on his smoking perisher, and rides the riffs of Mick's guitar in "Thunderbuck Ram." Soon the sounds and words of "I Can Feel" are washing over him as he sips and thoughts unbidden turn to his Moira: unconscious and alone in her hospital room, connected to machines with blinking lights keeping her breathing, alive but with no life as she wastes away in her bed so yes, Ian, I can feel too but she can't with her angry red bed sores and the former glory of her hair greasy and lifeless and the doctors want to know when, when, when…but he can't, even knowing he should and so he swallows more assuagement from the bottomless bottle somehow half-empty and the tape, like his lovely, his loved, his very love, is played through.

Groaning, he hoists himself out of the chair and, staggering a bit, makes his way to the stereo to rip out the tape. The shim falls to the floor. When he bends over to pick it up, so does he.

Weeping, he curls over onto his side and his body is wracked over and over. Eventually the sobbing subsides and he gathers himself, the tape and shim, and gets up. He returns *Mad Shadow* and its adjustor to their proper places and comes back to the tape deck with *The Hoople* (3). He inserts it along with the proper shim and returns to his seat. After "The Golden Age of Rock 'n' Roll" courses through at ninety-six decibels and the bottle has been emptied, "Marionette," one of his favorites, plays. Since first hearing its searing guitar licks and pounding piano as an adolescent, he's been fascinated by marionettes. Even though he's usually poor at memorizing lyrics, he knows all the words to this one.

Head weaving, eyes blurring, he sings along with Ian Hunter and the boys in the band, slurring the verses.

Singing is feeling; feeling is crying; crying is exhausting. The celebration has become an exercise in melancholy. His eyes are two rills and his nostrils are leaking snot. His face is a wretched mess; it badly needs cleaning so he bends forward in his chair to reach behind and get the folded bandanna lodged in his rear pocket (for at least two weeks). It's stuck in there so he leans even more and as he tugs the soiled red rag free he tumbles out of his chair. It is so lovely to be on the floor. He rolls on to his back, wipes his face clean with his filthy bandanna and considers it amazing how comfortable it is lying here. Just before passing out, his eyes find his poster, on the ceiling, of the Silver Surfer with his arms outstretched, balanced on his board and flying through the cosmos, exclaiming, "AT LAST…I AM **FREE!**"

※ ※ ※

A golden ingot of sunlight crawls through a crack in the curtains of the east facing window of the music room and onto the recumbent puppet master's lean thighs. The luminescent quadrilateral slowly sweeps across his angular hips, the crotch of his urine-soaked jeans, and on to the stained t-shirt clinging to the hollow of his ribs and protruding clavicles. It finds the knot of his Adam's apple and exposes, like a latter-day Katherine Hepburn sans scarf, the stark tendons of his attenuated neck then climbs over the gray stubble field poking out of the lunar landscape of his chin. When it reaches his thin, parched lips with tiny, smelt scales of skin drying between the cracks and white flecks nesting in the corners, he flinches and groans. Slowly, it rises on to the bristles of his upper lip and discovers the philtrum's shadowy crescent then, inexorably forward to the twin caves of his nostrils blaring their siren snore. The jaundiced bar, filled with motes engaged in a stately sarabande, ascends to the tip of his nose to find a red and swollen excrescence, a white pip in its summit. This, at age sixty, is so much a regular occurrence for Kyle he is certain he will be lying in his casket for the viewing with an angry scarlet blotch—begging to be squeezed—somewhere on his nose. The aureate parallelogram, long and narrow, crosses over to the bridge of his nose and slowly descends. It undulates up and over two sleep-swollen purses, is lost momentarily in the wrinkles of his lower lids, burns through the lashes until, finally, the sharp point of the leading angle stabs into the slit of his right eye. Both eyes pop open and with a moan he jerks his head into shade. Spluttering oaths, he snakes forward a few inches along the floor using scapulae and elbows to escape the fiery light. He closes his eyes and groans, wants to sleep more but it's too late.

He's awake and his head feels like during the night it got caught in the coupling mechanism of two fully loaded freight cars. It should be a jelly of brain, bone fragments, and blood but somehow is still intact. His mouth tastes like the exhaust stack of the diesel engine pulling those railroad cars. He rolls on to his side, gets up on his elbow, opens his eyes cautiously and sees the sunlight slicing across his torso. The dust motes floating in it are doing a courtly dance and he is fascinated by their bowing and twirling, their artful slides, dignified skips, mannered swirlings, graceful glissades. One silvered particulate captures his attention. It is in the shape of an upside-down "T" and seems to rise and fall of its own volition, flying back and forth, orbiting the dance partners. Capricious and willful, it eventually zooms out of the universe of sunlight and is lost to the surrounding shadows.

He collapses and, seeing nullity, stares at the ceiling. Despite his throbbing head, the wet burning in his crotch, and a mouth that is a foul and desiccated wasteland, he finally finds, in the depths of his hangover, some moxie and comes to the decision he has avoided for weeks.

Sitting up is John Henry driving railroad spikes through his head. Bile rises and it takes all his willpower to hold back the vomit. He gets to his feet slowly. With head down, left hand cupped and shading his eyes, right hand out to steady himself, Kyle staggers into the bathroom to shower, brush his teeth, and swallow a few mouthfuls of water and several acetaminophen. After dressing in his most comfortable old jeans and a soft, warm flannel shirt, he gets a bucket of water with pine-sol and some rags and cleans the urine from the carpeting in the music room as best he can while listening to Boz Skaggs' *Silk Degree*.

By the time he's done with the cleaning and Boz's ultra-smooth tune "Harbor Lights," he's feeling nearly human and can finally tolerate some eggs, toast and orange juice. After breakfast he does the dishes from yesterday and this morning including his whiskey tumbler. He wonders why he hardly ever cleans this particular glass; it's not like him, he always keeps up with dirty dishes.

After washing the last item, he releases the greasy water, wipes the sink and counters clean, dries his hands, then calls the hospital to rendezvous with the doctor during her rounds on the Intensive Care Unit in the afternoon. He has the day off; tomorrow starts rehearsals for *The Death of Tintagiles* at the puppet theater. The boss wants him to play the lead.

Kyle has to finish up a few final tasks for the marionettes. A perfectionist by nature, he wants every detail with his figures correct when he brings them to the theater tomorrow. First, he makes a pot of coffee. The smell of the fresh brewed, restorative is divine. He likes it strong and black and drinks it from a large white ceramic mug.

He takes another drink. It is still very good but he thinks it would be even better with a splash of brandy—not too much, it would never do to arrive at the hospital a drunken mess but a little nip would steady his nerves for the most difficult thing he has ever had to do. He finds the fifth of Camus VSOP cognac in the back of the cabinet over the stove. He and the wife got it—he can't remember from whom—as an anniversary gift years ago. They reserve it for special guests and it is still three-quarters full after all these years but there is no point in saving it any longer so he pours a jigger into his mug, takes a sip. It is very tasty but another half shot would improve the taste of his coffee significantly without impairing his functioning in the least so in it goes. He caps the bottle, leaves it on the counter, takes another drink of the adulterated joe, and, from deep in his throat, hums appreciation for the concoction. On the way downstairs he's wondering why he didn't try this long ago.

The first thing to do is to suck flame to the end of an unfiltered then flick on the bench grinder. Once it is at full rpms, he takes the fancy letter opener to the fine wheel and, with sparks flying off in ocher fireworks, sharpens both edges. Algovale's sword is finished about the same time as the cigarette.

※ ※ ※

He wants to test the controls for the lead character and the rest of the marionettes before taking them into Detroit tomorrow but his cup is empty and he's feeling the need for more dark roast. After a trip upstairs for a high octane refill, this time with two jiggers of the cognac—with another half shot just for luck (not to worry, he can handle his liquor)—and another butt, he returns to the basement. While going up and down the steps he feels a dull pain in his right foot and tries to put as little weight on it as possible. As an older man, he is familiar with these sudden, inexplicable twinges in various parts of his body.

Many years ago, Kyle had built a portable puppet stage to take to city parks or shopping mall courts for him and Moira to do marionette performances. After they were hired on by the Detroit Puppet Company, the stage was made a permanent fixture at the end of the basement opposite the work bench area and used by them for rehearsal and practicing motions, especially ones demanded by new productions and figures. Carrying his cup of java, he limps over to the stage, turns on the bank of stage lights, both spotlights, and quaffs more coffee before setting the cup on top of the back rail of the puppeteer's bridge.

One of the 40-watt incandescent bulbs for the stage lights is burned out so he removes it then shakes it close to his ear so he can hear the filaments tinkling inside and know it is a problem with the bulb and not the fixture. He returns to the work desk, tosses the dead bulb in the trash can, and is irritated to discover he only has those stupid, energy efficient but dim fluorescent light bulbs with the curving tubes mandated by our overreaching government. He approaches the proscenium with its burgundy paint chipped and damaged from years of use and its overarching banner: The Pluperfect Puppet Playhouse, still readable despite the peeling gilt. He leans in through the open, plush purple velour curtains faded with age, pushes two of the several blocks of wood of various dimensions for practicing seating motions to one side and the four-step riser for practicing stair-climbing to the other side, then slides his hips on to the stage so he can reach up and put in the new bulb.

How many puppeteers does it take to screw in a light bulb? Just one, when it's scripted into the final act of the play.

His eyes catch the stage right spotlight and are blinded momentarily. Blinking, blinking, he sits on the scratched, worn floorboards, the site of so many memorable scenes with his wife by his side creating magic with their puppets for countless young audiences. Their favorite play was *Sleeping Beauty*. He loved the moment when Prince Florimond kisses the Sleeping Beauty…

The morning light, diffused through the gauzy linen curtains of the bedroom window, illuminates the exquisite face of his bride next to him. On her side, facing him, her head is resting on her hands which are together as in prayer. The tableau, framed by the snowy pillow, is so perfect it seems posed by a photographer but, for her, this is a favored way of sleeping.

Her full, dark lashes lie still against the uppermost curves of her flawless cheeks. A long lock, walnut and rich with copper highlights, has strayed from under the sheets and draped itself over her short, little nose. Not wishing to disturb her, he tenderly, carefully brushes aside the tendril of hair with the tips of his fingers. His eyes devour her sleeping loveliness and he is baffled at how such beauty as this can possibly love him.

After several moments, he is compelled to kiss what he is certain is the cutest nose on the planet. When his lips barely brush it, she awakens with a languorous sigh, opens her bottomless, earthen brown eyes, blesses him, though unaware it is such, with a sleepy half smile and murmurs, "What?"

He has no words, only a gazing in mute adoration.

Still speechless, he desires the sound of her laughter, a music of the heavens for his ears. With an inspired, unexplainable, and spontaneous silliness, he burrows under the blankets to butt his head, like a pup seeking affection, into her abdomen. She yelps in surprise, giggles as she pushes his head away. Though intuiting the answer, asks nevertheless, with a hint of sultriness, "What are you doing?"

He pops his head up, grinning but wordless still, to gaze again in mute adoration.

She laughs low and softly, opens her arms. Kyle slides into her embrace, buries his face in the curved space of neck and shoulder, the silken glory of her hair, and inhales the natural perfumes of her skin.

Outside, clouds part and the sun, a tyger's eye, burns brightly. A crack in the curtains forms an auric knife's edge across the lovers. Dust floating in the narrow aurora dances an allemande. Two gliding motes circle each other, come together and, clinging to each other, fall from the golden light...

His eyes are watery; tears are threatening to overspill but there has been more than enough crying. A past master of stuffing feelings like they are a down sleeping bag fitting into an emotional sack the size of a loaf of bread, he won't allow it and blinks them away. After placing the blocks and riser back in their usual places on the stage, he goes to the back rail, finishes his coffee and brandy, remembers with a smile, the time so long ago, when she woke him with a kiss on the oily monstrosity of his nose. For him, it was quite possibly the purest act of love he's ever known.

Again, he limps upstairs for a refill. He is sailing with one sheet to the wind now. Hoisting a second sheet, then a third, overrides any earlier concerns he had about appearances for his afternoon's meeting with Moira's doctor. This one is more cognac than coffee as the pot held only enough for a fourth of a cup. He returns the empty pot to the warmer and forgets to turn off the coffee-maker, then does a taste test and decides the mix is beyond good and he probably should have started drinking this years ago. By the time he returns the cup to its spot on the back rail it is half empty and the pain in his foot is all but forgotten.

He removes Ygraine and Bellangère from the cabinet and carries them over to the puppet stage, goes behind the proscenium, mounts the three steps to the puppeteer's bridge, hangs each from a hook on the back rail, returns to the cabinet, and does the same for Algovale and Tintagiles. The child marionette, for some odd reason, is considerably heavier than the three adult marionettes.

After warming his belly with another generous swallow of his coffee cocktail, he gets the sword from the work bench and brings it back stage. Swathed in alcohol-induced, holiday feelings of comfort and joy, focused on his creations and scarcely cognizant of his vegetative wife in the hospital, he takes Bellangère from the hook, places his right hand in the controller and stands her upright on the stage.

He goes through his usual final shake-down routine to make sure everything is perfect with his *poupée* before he takes it to work tomorrow. First is a visual inspection of wig, head, limbs, costume, and feet. Second is a series of motions to see how well synchronized the controller is with the figure. They include walking, sitting, climbing stairs, and what appears to be an entire, aerobics work-out to see how well every joint is working. As is usual with him, the marionette floats a bit too much when walking and one of her feet strikes at least one of the steps each time when mounting the practice stairs, but this is an operator's issue, movements he's never totally mastered.

He does the same run through with Ygraine. Her controller and strings are perfect. He has to remove a couple of loose threads from her costume and re-glue part of her wig before deeming her ready for the stage lights.

He reaches back for the cup and, forgetting it is empty, lifts it to his lip. A couple of drops tantalize his tongue. Infuriated, Kyle backhands the cup against the wall which assuages his rage but immediately leads to regret for destroying his favorite cup. He vents a short, sharp scream of frustration then calmly lifts Ygraine from the stage then hangs her on the back rail.

Kyle notes some dustiness, a certain aridity in his throat—the more he is in his cups the quicker this happens—so he struggles up the stairs once more for another refill. At the second step he bounces off the wall which sends him caroming off the stair rail at the third step and back to the wall on the fourth step where he stops for a moment to collect himself. With right hand extended to the wall and left hand firmly grasping the rail, he continues upward. At the top step, he stumbles and goes to all fours on the landing, hurts both knees and one of his wrists. Fortunately, it is the left one so he will still be able to operate the controller with his right. Rubbing his wrist and slightly stooped over from the pain in his knees, he staggers into the kitchen to discover the coffee pot has only a foul smelling, blackened residue in its bottom. He snatches it from the warmer, turns on the cold water at the kitchen sink and, not thinking things through, thrusts it under the faucet. The temperature differential results in some steam boiling up and a snapping sound as a crack forms along the side of the glass pot. His immediate recourse is to smash it against the sink which sends shards of hot glass flying. One pierces his little finger, another impales the baggy flesh under the lower lid of his right eye. He drops the remains of the pot in the sink and hurries to the bathroom.

After several minutes of first aid he has his two minor wounds, which, in his current condition, are not in the least painful, cleaned with rubbing alcohol (the burn tells him it is working) and bandaged. He returns to the kitchen. His head is suffering from two invisible wires stretching down from the shadows above to pierce his skull at the temples and insert themselves into his brain. Recurrent since he was an adolescent, they are always tightly strung and horrendously painful, a controlling torment with demands impossible to ignore. His palliation, the only way to sever the strings for immediate relief, is a drink. Bourbon seems to work best although cognac, he's discovering, is nearly as efficacious. He finds his favorite tumbler drying in the dish rack and fills it with the remaining Camus, takes a sip.

Back in his basement workshop, after putting Algovale through its paces, he determines the right shoulder string has to be lengthened just a bit. The left knee and hip and right elbow are also too tight. The repairs are easy enough but by the time he has all three joints working smoothly much of the contents of his tumbler has evaporated—the only reasonable explanation because he certainly doesn't remember drinking them.

The hilt of the sword is placed into Algovale's right fist and Kyle has the old man wave it around, execute a thrust and parry, a lunge, and a riposte. All of the moves are awkward but this is due to operator issues not faults in the marionette. He takes the sharpened letter opener and, as if it's a miniature version of Excalibur, stabs into a block, as if that's a cubical, wooden stone of Camelot.

Hanging the old man on his hook is a matter of trial and error. Going through the process slowly and carefully, he succeeds on the third attempt and tells himself it's a problem with the hook which he will have to replace tomorrow, or the next day, or never.

In one swift movement, he sweeps the tumbler from its resting place, tips it to his lips, and takes a swallow, takes another, tries for a third unsuccessfully as his tongue is again tantalized by the last drops. With the tawny liquor still flaming in throat and belly, he is off a bit when he tries to return the tumbler to its place on the back rail. It falls and smashes into pieces. Frowning, he leans over the back rail and inspects, with bleary disappointment, the shards littering the floor, figures he'll clean up those along with the cup fragments tomorrow, or the next day, or never.

Straightening up too quickly causes some dizziness and he pivots stage left, staggers a bit, tilts into the front rail. Kyle grabs both rails to keep from falling, widens his stance
for better balance, closes his eyes, drops his head, shakes it a few times until the spinning stops. After a few moments of deep breathing, he feels steady and able to finish the morning's tasks with a final run through for Tintagiles.

He opens his eyes and stares at the scuffed stage floor another moment or two before lifting his head and turning it to look at the child puppet. His eyes widen in disbelief as he sees it hanging there—so lifelike it has to be breathing—shaking its head at him, its features twisted with disgust, its eyes mordant and angry.

Frightened, his arm partially extended in a warding gesture and blinking rapidly, the image of Tintagiles shutters through a succession of changes like a Kodak Carousel slide projector from demonic back to beatific.

With his heart racing, breathing rapid and shallow, he drops to his knees, leans forward until nose-to-nose with his ultimate creation suspended and perfectly still with its green eyes staring straight ahead. Kyle stands, removes it from the hook. Holding it by the back of the neck in his left hand, arm extended, he examines it head to toe and from every angle. The countenance is without flaw, the best he's ever done, the expression innocent, calm but with gravitas rather than the naiveté of his original intention. The figure's mass is startling. Its heaviness, though inexplicable, will allow for greater control as he inserts his right hand into the controller and tries a few preliminary motions on the stage floor.

He walks the marionette across the stage and back. The realism of this most complex of motions is nothing less than astonishing. This is, by far, the best Kyle has ever operated a puppet. Tintagiles is so solid on his feet yet fluid he might as well be an actual living being. Head, shoulders, arms, hands, hips, knees, and feet are synchronized and in miraculous harmony as the *fantoche* struts around the stage confidently, proudly.

Kyle wants to try Tintagiles on the riser and starts him back across the stage but it's as if the marionette can read his mind. After the first couple of steps, the figure appears to be a free agent moving of its own volition. The operator has to work to keep up. Half way across, Tintagiles, in unexpected exuberance, hops, skips twice, and does a bow to the non-existent audience. Kyle, lost in a dense fog of brandy fumes, is frowning in concentration, not sure if those were planned motions. Did his hands do them of their own accord? Is there a disconnect between them and his drenched brain? How was it accomplished when it seemed the strings were so loosely curved at times while at other times, and equally as impossible, there was tugging at the strings?

Tintagiles, assured and purposeful, if not jaunty, continues to the riser, ascends, turns around, then descends the four steps with alacrity and, striding with purpose, makes toward the opposite end of the stage. Midway there Kyle stops to pull his bandanna from his left rear pocket and mop the sweat from his face and brow. He is dazed by the incredible perfection of every motion of the marionette. He has never been this good as a puppeteer. Nobody, not even Ronnie Burkett or Erico Chizzy, has this skill level.

When he's done and the red, paisley cloth is back in his pocket, he looks down to see Tintagiles' head has fallen backwards so it appears to be looking up at him and the expression seems to be one of suspicion and anger. Kyle quickly checks the positioning of the head strings on the crossbar of his controller. Everything, even in his drunken confusion, appears in good order and when he looks back at his marionette it is, as it should be, staring straight ahead.

Kyle is thinking it is time to do a scene or two with Tintagiles as was earlier practiced with his sisters to allow for gesticulations and dramatic flourishing. Using Ygraine's contralto and a soft, childish lisping for Tintagiles, he chooses the middle of Act III with Ygraine and Tintagiles in their apartment:

>T: You too, you are sad, sister Ygraine…
>
>Y: No, no, you can see I am smiling…
>
>T: And my other sister too…
>
>Y: No, she is smiling too…
>
>T: That is not a smile…I know…
>
>Y: Come, kiss me and think of other things…
>
>T: What other things, sister Ygraine?…Why do you hurt me when you kiss me?
>
>Y: I hurt you?

T: Yes...I do not know why I hear your heart beating, sister Ygraine...

Y: You hear it beating?

T: Oh, oh, it is beating, it is beating, as if it would...

Y: Would what?

T: I do not know, sister Ygraine.

Y: There is no need to be frightened without reason, or talk in riddles...Look! Your eyes are wet...Why are you troubled? I hear your heart too...You always hear it when you kiss like this...Then it speaks and says things the tongue does not know...

There are more lines to this scene. He wants to get to where Tintagiles cries, "I heard...Them...They are coming!" but he is again perspiring copiously and his vision is blurred from sweat dripping into his eyes. While still holding the controller and wrist string, he takes turns quickly wiping them with each cuff of his flannel shirt. Tintagiles mirrors these motions by wiping his tears—which are, of course, impossible for a marionette—with the sleeves of his nightshirt. The tears are either a trick of the light or, more likely, drops of perspiration that fell from the operator on to his face.

Further clearing his vision with rapid blinking, Kyle, to finish the rehearsal with Tintagiles, switches to the latter part of Act V, shortly after Ygraine's nihilistic monologue acted out earlier. In this scene the child is locked behind a great iron door and his sister is desperately trying to open it before the evil queen destroys her beloved brother:

T: No, no, there is nothing…I can find nothing at all…I can not see the little chink of light any more…

Y: What is it Tintagiles…I can hardly hear…

T: Little sister, sister Ygraine. It can not be done now…

Y: What is it, Tintagiles!…Where are you going?…

T: She is there!…I have no more courage.— Sister Ygraine, sister Ygraine!…I can feel her!…

Y: Who?…Who?…

T: I do not know…I can not see…But it can not be done now!…

The lines, particularly the last one, resonate in Kyle's reeling brain and he recalls what must be done later today. The emotional pain is too much and the practice is halted as he, still holding the controller and wrist string in either hand, rests the heels of his palms on the front rail, locks his arms, and bows his head with eyes closed.

The strings are slack but Tintagiles, who, according to the play, should now be enfeebled, stands straight and tall. He again does the unthinkable and slowly, deliberately, gazes defiantly upward at what has been controlling him. This creature, a huge and looming black presence, is in the shadows created by the footlights. It must be the Queen. He can't remember how he got here but he must be in the enormous tower where she lives. His mind is a kaleidoscopic confusion of images; most of them relate to pain and entrapment but he does recall Ygraine's echoing words from when he, although unable to picture either now, arrived at the island and first saw the dark castle:

> *...that is where the Queen sits on her throne...she does not show herself...She lives there in the tower alone; and those who serve her do not go out in the day...She is grown very old; she is the mother of our mother and only wants to reign alone...She is jealous and suspicious, and they say she is mad...She fears someone will rise to her place...Her orders are obeyed but no one knows how...They say she is not beautiful and has grown enormous...But those who have seen her dare not speak now...She has a power that no one understands...And we live with a great weight upon our soul...*

This lurking evil threatens him and those he loves; he knows what must be done and has the moxie, dear father, to do it! He stalks over to grasp Algovale's sword stuck upright in a wooden block...

Kyle straightens, opens his eyes, extends his arms and the lines stretch from controller to *poupée*. He wants to finish the run through by walking Tintagiles to a block and practice seating motions. The steps are firm, flawless and, even though his forearms and shoulders are starting to fatigue, he continues to marvel at how well he is operating except, to his utter bafflement, the marionette, tugging at the strings, marches past the block Kyle had in mind and goes to the one with the impaled sword…

Tintagiles, like a young Arthur, pulls the sword. He senses the Queen is stunned at his shocking defiance. He knows he only has a few seconds before the monstrosity above recovers her wits and calls for her guards. In one swift motion he slices through the back string attached to his waist. Both hands will be needed to climb up to where she lurks. He places the sword in his mouth as if it's a scimitar and he's a buccaneer and the strings that once controlled him are now a ship's shrouds. Though a third her size, the dauntless hero reaches behind, grasps the dangling back string, pulls it forward and starts climbing upwards, hand-over-hand, rapidly...

Kyle watches in drunken stupefaction as the puppet reaches out and grasps the sharpened letter opener with fingers that can't move, cuts the back string with it, places Algovale's sword in a toothless mouth that can't hold it, then, like one of the pirates from the production of *Peter Pan* they did years ago, starts clambering up the string. His sodden mind is trying to comprehend. Is he hallucinating? Has his marionette come to life? Is it actually moving of its own volition? It reaches the top of the back string and steps on to the front rail. Separated by only eighteen inches, they are virtually eye-to-eye. Balanced and sure-footed, staring at him, its once perfect features are twisted into an expression of pure hatred and rage as it removes the breakable dirk from its mouth and, like an Olympic-caliber fencer, lunges forward…

Tintagiles reaches the top of the string, slides easily over to a rail waist-high with the huge Queen. Now that he is out of the footlights he can see she is even more hideous than imagined. Her face is lined with age, scarred and pock marked, so ugly it seems more of a man's than a woman's. She is dazed, motionless as he takes the sword from his mouth. He lunges forward so swiftly the evil queen doesn't duck her head, only has time to widen her eyes giving him an even better target. The blade penetrates the pupil of the right eye, slices through the brain stem, pierces the cerebellum, impales the back of the skull. The hilt and his hand are awash in aqueous humor and blood as a bolt of agony forks through his own right eye. He loses his footing in a slippery splash of gore and the blade breaks off as the mannish Queen collapses to the floor of the puppeteer's bridge. Tintagiles plummets from the rail, fractured sword in hand, and strikes the planks of the stage floor head first caving in his fragile skull. The force of the fall causes his body to roll and limbs to flail while the giant lying next to him twitches twice then quietly expires...

The footlights shine on. In the brightness, Tintagiles lies on his back with his right leg twisted underneath him, his left leg at a right angle to his broken hip, his left arm is akimbo while his right has somehow convolved so that the haft of the sword, still clutched in his right fist, is protruding from the middle of what remains of the right side of his face.

With his remains in the shadows, Kyle's right arm has fallen across the bridge and into the light. His right hand is encased in the controller and the strings have managed to become entangled as his fingertips brush against Tintagiles contorted shoulder.

There is a drip, drip of blood falling from the front rail. It splatters on the stage as the roiled dust, luminous in the spotlights, begins a solemn passacaglia sweeping slowly downward to settle upon the recumbent forms of master and puppet, puppet and master.

Also From *Translucent Eyes Press*

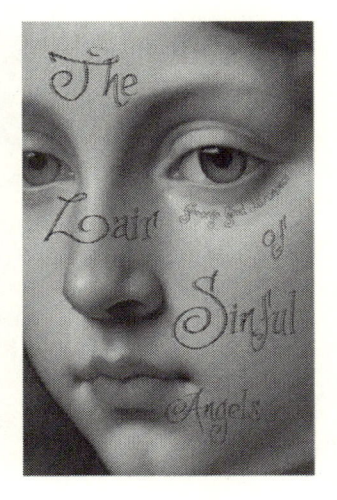

TRANSLUCENT EYES PRESS

Made in the USA
Columbia, SC
02 October 2024